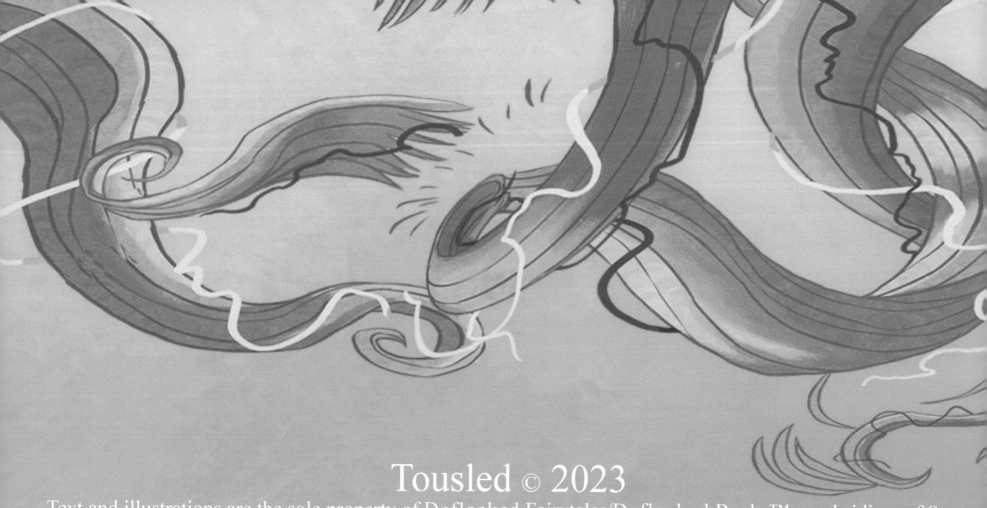

Tousled © 2023

ISBN # 979-8-9898830-2-8 (Hardcover)
ISBN # 979-8-9898830-3-5 (Paperback)
Published in the US by DeFlocked Books™

www.DeflockedFairytales.com

DeFlocked
FairyTales
DeFlockedFairytales.com

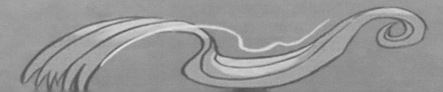

Tousled

Story By:

Rooney Lennon

Art By:

Andy Catling

For Aunt Eileen, who lived and loved well.
I carry you with me.

And to Danny,
My patient partner in crazy adventures.
Thank you so much for bringing my
imagination and dream to life on these pages.

Once upon a time, there lived a girl of eight or nine,

with rosy cheeks,

a musical laugh,

a fiery spirit, and a love of giraffes.

Sunny lived her life without a care, except when it came to taming her hair...

A little bit **springy**,

a tiny bit STRAIGHT,

she never knew what it would do on any given day.

Would it STICK up all over or would it behave?

Sunny was happy to leave it alone, she didn't care about brushes, detanglers or combs.

But her mom looked upon it like a wild and free horse, she didn't want to break, but ride without force.

They braided it up
to take on the town,

but by evening less of it was up than was down.

With it came sticks, bird's nests, and a guppy.

One time it even brought home a puppy.

They cut it all off but it grew even faster,

and almost in spite,
became more a disaster.

Sunny was happy with her thick golden tresses,

**that her friends used to jump rope
in their sweet little dresses.**

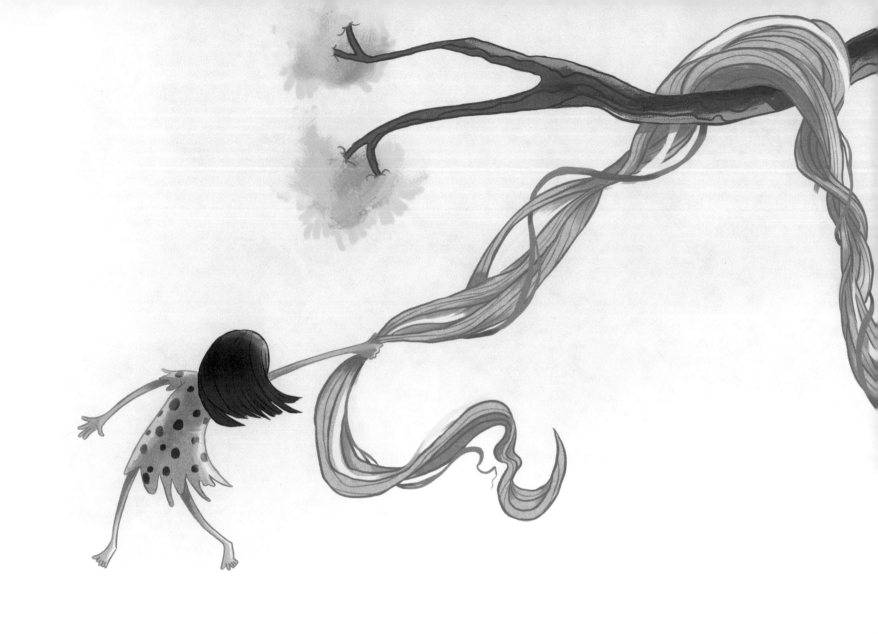

It made a great vine to swing like Tarzan

or fly through the air like Peter Pan.

It was the perfect rope to climb high towers,

or decorate with flowers for hours and hours, when the sun didn't shine because of rain showers.

She loved that it made her stand apart and how grown-ups would walk by and smile.

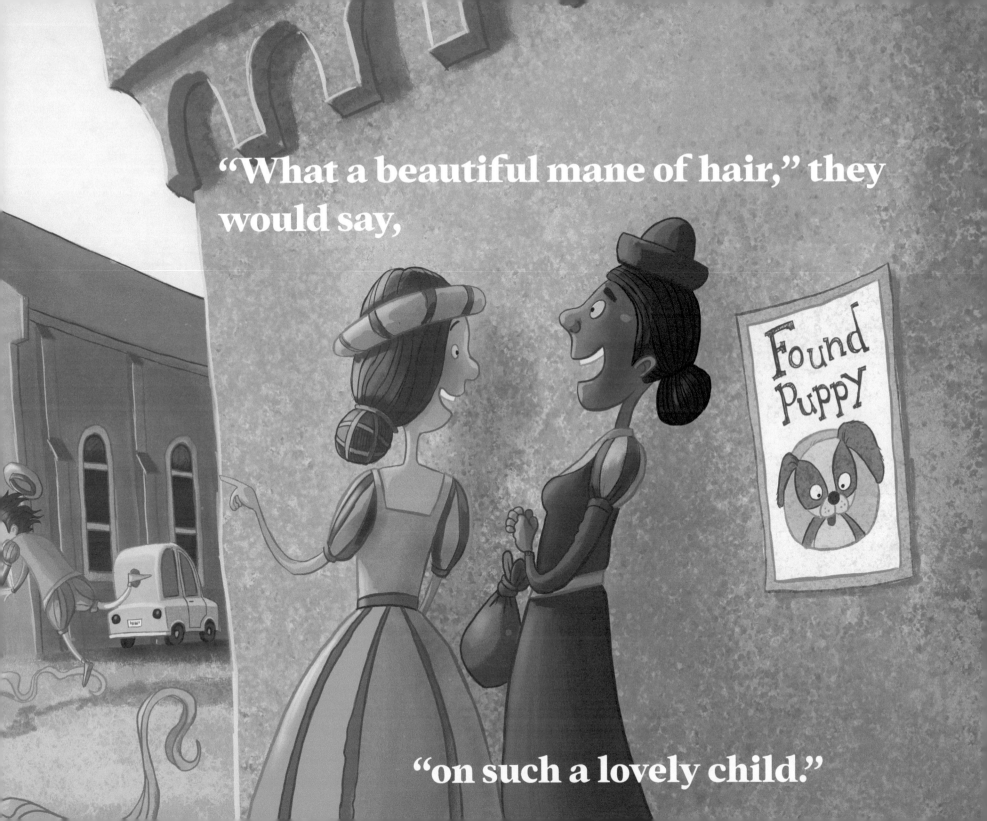

"What a beautiful mane of hair," they would say,

"on such a lovely child."

**Sunny's pride for her hair was strong,
and she held her head high all day long,**

as her poor mom just tried to hold on;

The war of the hair and the pride of the mane
could've gone on for years and all been in vain;

If Sunny kept missing her hair's subtle cues that there was something greater she was meant to do.

But one day at the hair salon, when Sunny's mom was under a dryer, Sunny grew antsy and tired of waiting and started reading a flyer.

On it were pictures of children whose heads were completely bald. And they each had a sparkle that made them special and beautiful and Sunny found herself enthralled.

There were places to donate her hair that would make the most beautiful wigs.

Sunny loved the idea of sharing her gift and bringing joy to other kids.

Now every few months Sunny wakes up early, ready for the salon. And no one could be prouder (and a bit relieved) of their daughter than her loving mom.

With a SNIP

and a CHOP

it doesn't hurt, not a DROP.

And her hair never fails to grow back quickly, just as healthy and strong.

**Sunny still loves her long locks
and how wild and free they flow.**

But often giving to others helps us mature and grow.

Sunny now knows that it's not her hair that makes her stand apart.

What makes a person glow from the inside out
is what they choose to do with their heart.

THE END

Rooney Lennon fell in love with words at age four. At five, she was featured in the local paper as a "super reader". That same year, she wrote her first children's book and at age six, her first series. As a grown up, she taught creative writing to kiddos in Oregon and California, where she hopes to have inspired future writers and imaginers. When she's not creating adventures with words, she enjoys spontaneous outbursts of song, looking for mermaids at the beach and fairies in the forest. She lives in San Diego, California, with an ark's worth of expressive animals, her novelist daughter, and an enterprising husband.

Andy Catling is a professional illustrator with more than 70 titles under his belt. He has worked for many publishers, including Oxford University Press, Caterpillar Books, Quarto, Harper, Lion Hudson, and others in the UK and around the world. Andy loves illustrating picture books and books for older children using a more mature style. If a story has dragons, knights, pirates, monsters or the like, then Andy will want to illustrate it!

Andy lives in Hampshire in the UK where he spends his time, well, illustrating.

Printed in the USA
CPSIA information can be obtained
at www.ICGtesting.com
JSHW040743260224
57921JS00008B/95